The Sunday Blues

A book for schoolchildren, schoolteachers, and anybody else who dreads Monday mornings

First published in Great Britain by Hodder Children's Books, London

Copyright © 2001 by Neal Layton

First U.S. edition 2002

Library of Congress Cataloging-in-Publication Data is available.

Library of Congress Catalog Card Number 2002023372

ISBN 0-7636-1975-2

10 9 8 7 6 5 4 3 2 1

Printed in Hong Kong

This book was typeset in Officina Serif.
The illustrations were done in collage, ink, and Photoshop.

Candlewick Press
2067 Massachusetts Avenue
Cambridge, Massachusetts 02140

visit us at www.candlewick.com

The Sunday Blues

Neal Layton

CANDLEWICK PRESS
CAMBRIDGE, MASSACHUSETTS

It was Sunday, and Steve was fed up.

He was fed up because it was Sunday
and because that meant tomorrow was Monday
and because that meant SCHOOL!

SCHOOL BOOKS

SCHOOL LUNCHES

SCHOOL CLOTHES

Steve's dad suggested they all go for a walk after lunch.

On the walk, Steve

... splashed in puddles,

found a giant snail,

ran around with their dog, Benny,

and generally had a fantastic time!

"Why don't we stop in at Auntie Vera's on the way back?" suggested Steve's mom.

Steve liked Auntie Vera.

Maybe visiting Auntie Vera wasn't such a good idea.

Going home, Steve got really sad because it was school the next day. He would miss Benny and Mom and Dad . . .

. . . and he was sure he'd have a terrible day there,
because school was really, really, really horrible.

When they got home, it was fish sticks, french fries, and baked beans for dinner. *Yummeroony!* Steve's favorite!

There was even Jell-O and ice cream to follow.
Double mega yummeroony!
But Steve had forgotten something else that
happened on Sundays . . .

After his bath, Steve's dad read a really exciting story about pirates.

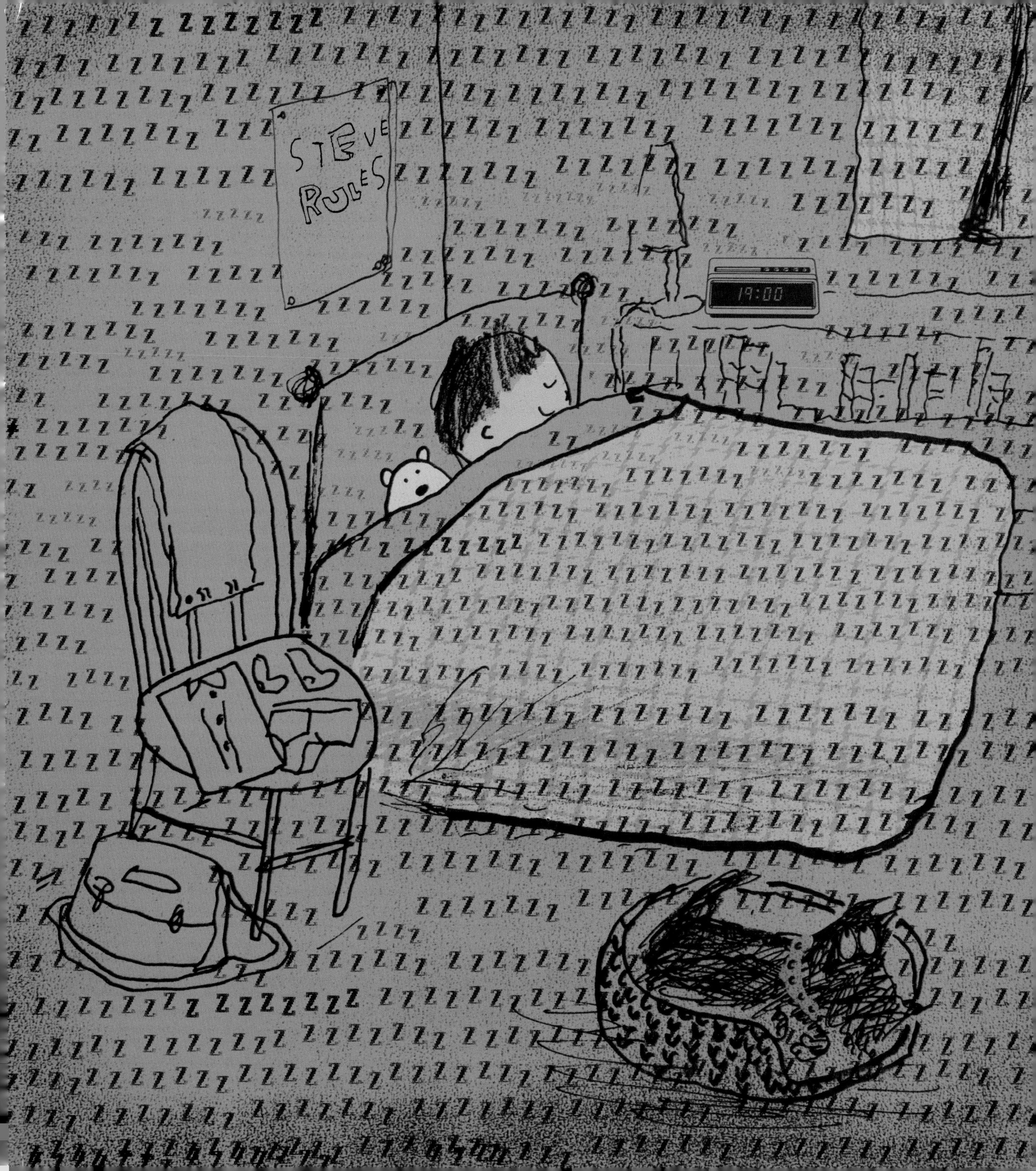
STEVE RULES
19:00

That night, Steve had lots of dreams . . .

...and then he woke up.

It was Monday morning.

Steve got up, got dressed, and
very, very slowly plodded downstairs.

He had breakfast.   He kissed his dad goodbye.

He got in the car.
This was it.

There was no escape.

The moment he had been dreading all Sunday had finally arrived. It was time for school.

At the gate, Steve could see his school friends in the playground, waiting for the bell to ring.

Mark was playing soccer. Dave and Tanya
were looking at books.

Tim, Sarah, and Stacey were playing jump rope.
Gary was doing handstands.

Steve said goodbye to his mom and joined his friends in the playground.

Maybe school wasn't so bad after all!

Days of the Week

Saturday

Sunday

Monday

Tuesday

Wedesday

Thursday

Fri

mandag
tirsdag
onsdag
torsdag
fredag
lørdag
søndag

DIMANCHE
LUDI
RDI
CUDI
NOREDI
MEDI

Montag
Dienstag
Mittwoch
Donnerstag
Freitag
Samstag (Sonnabend)
Sonntag

0 1 2 3 4 5 6

JAPAN
FOR GENERAL WRITING
SINCE 1913
0199190058

YELLOW